# PILOBOLUS

## THE HUMAN ALPHABET

### PHOTOGRAPHS BY JOHN KANE

ROARING BROOK PRESS
NEW MILFORD, CONNECTICUT

## DANCERS

Rebecca Anderson, Adam Battelstein, Sandy Chase, Otis Cook, Josie Coyoc, Eric Dunlap, Mark Fucik, Renée Jaworski, Rebecca Jung, Gaspard Louis, Jennifer Macavinta, Tamieca McCloud, Emily Milam, Rebecca Stenn, and introducing Max B. Raven Cook.

COSTUMES: Lawrence Casey.

CHOREOGRAPHY by Robby Barnett, Alison Chase, Michael Tracy, and Jonathan Wolken.

Copyright © 2005 by Pilobolus, Inc.
Photographs copyright © 2005 by John Kane

Published by Roaring Brook Press
Roaring Brook Press is a division of Holtzbrinck Publishing Holdings Limited Partnership
143 West Street, New Milford, Connecticut 06776

Distributed in Canada by H. B. Fenn and Company Ltd.

Library of Congress Cataloging-in-Publication Data
The human alphabet / by Pilobolus ; photographs by John Kane.
    p. cm.
1. English language-Alphabet-Juvenile literature. 2. Body, Human-Pictorial works-Juvenile literature. I. Kane, John. II. Pilobolus Dance Theatre.
PE1155.H84 2005
428.1_3-dc22
2004065052

ISBN: 1-59643-066-4

Roaring Brook Press books are available for special promotions and premiums.
For details, contact: Director of Special Markets, Holtzbrinck Publishers.

First Edition September 2005
Printed in China
10 9 8 7 6 5 4 3 2 1

BOOK DESIGN BY MOLLY LEACH

**HERE**
are 26
letters of
the alphabet
and 26 pictures—
all made of people!
Can you guess what
each picture shows?

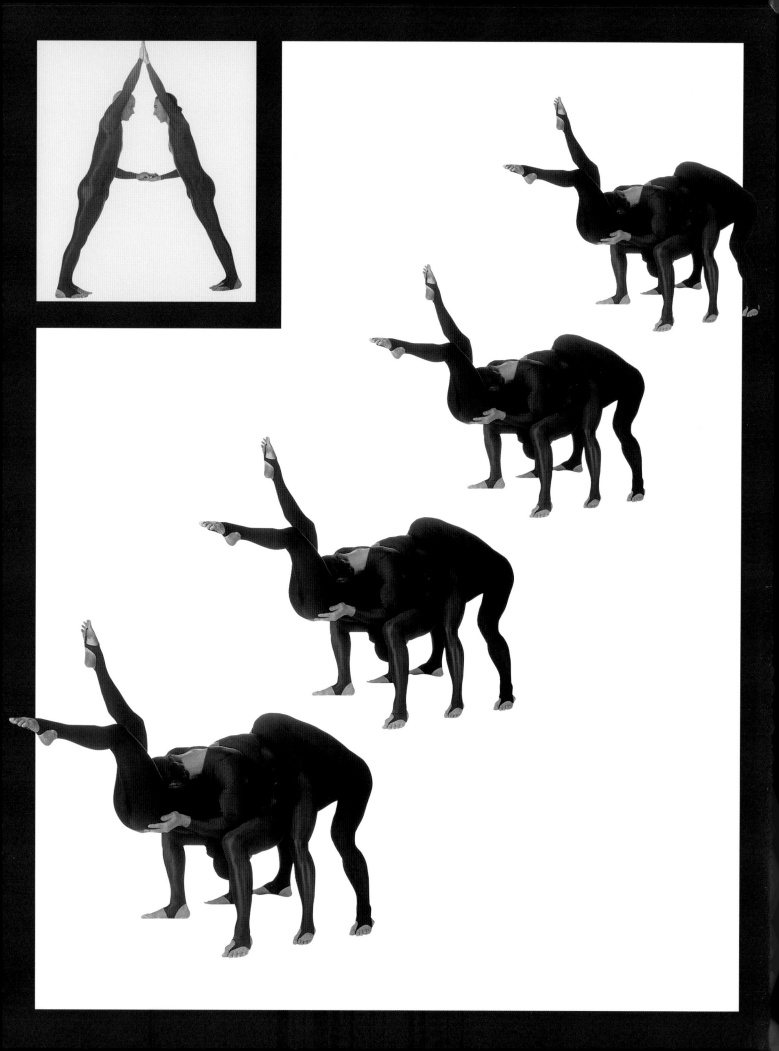

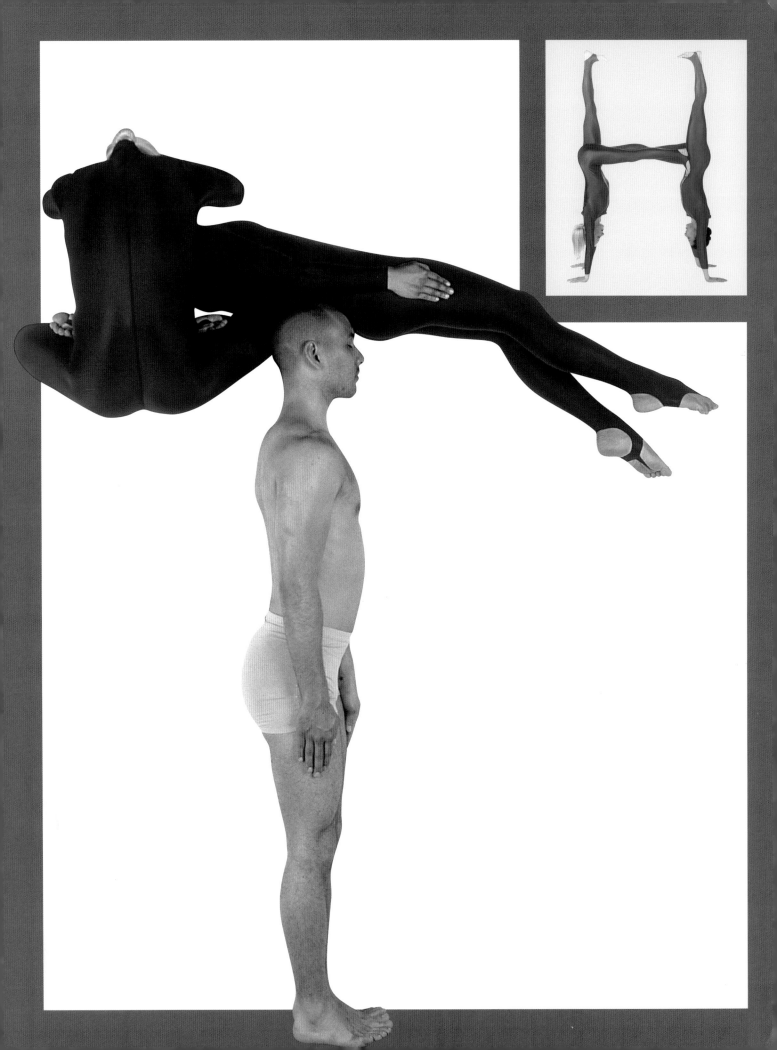

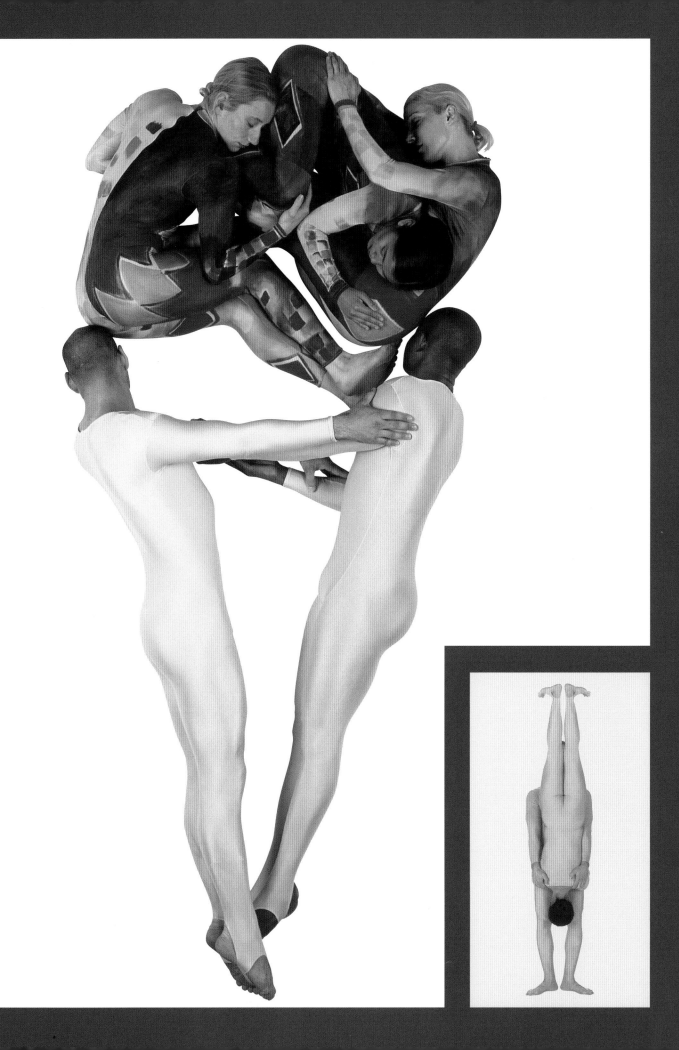

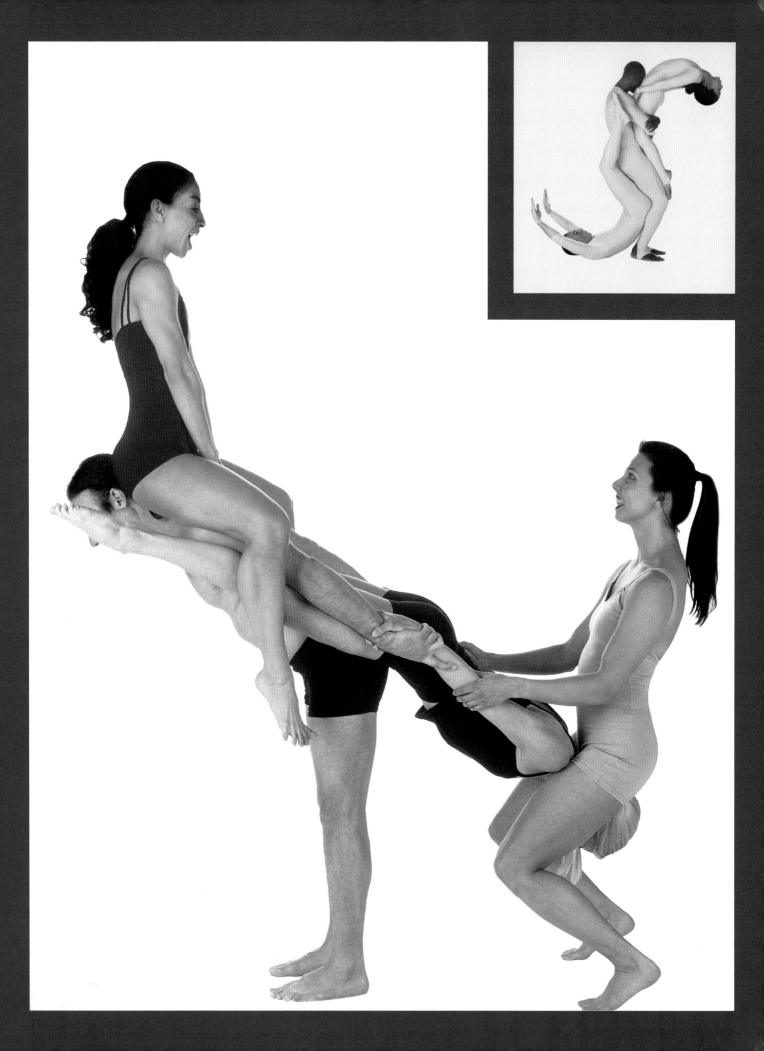

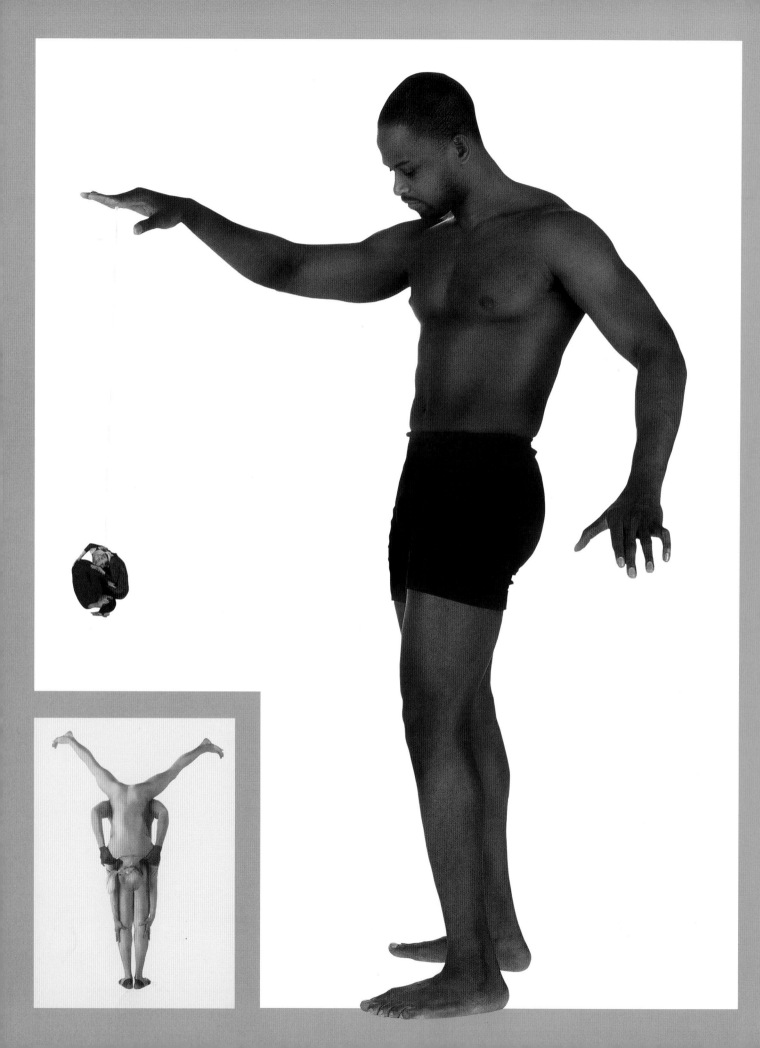

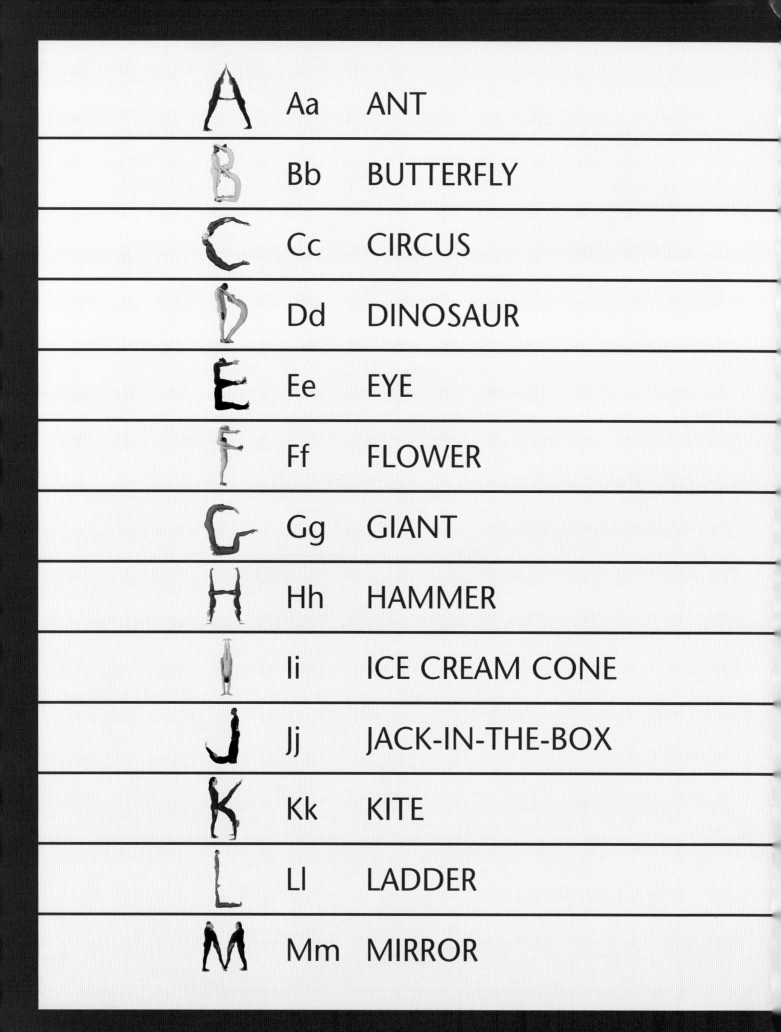

| | | |
|---|---|---|
| Aa | ANT |
| Bb | BUTTERFLY |
| Cc | CIRCUS |
| Dd | DINOSAUR |
| Ee | EYE |
| Ff | FLOWER |
| Gg | GIANT |
| Hh | HAMMER |
| Ii | ICE CREAM CONE |
| Jj | JACK-IN-THE-BOX |
| Kk | KITE |
| Ll | LADDER |
| Mm | MIRROR |

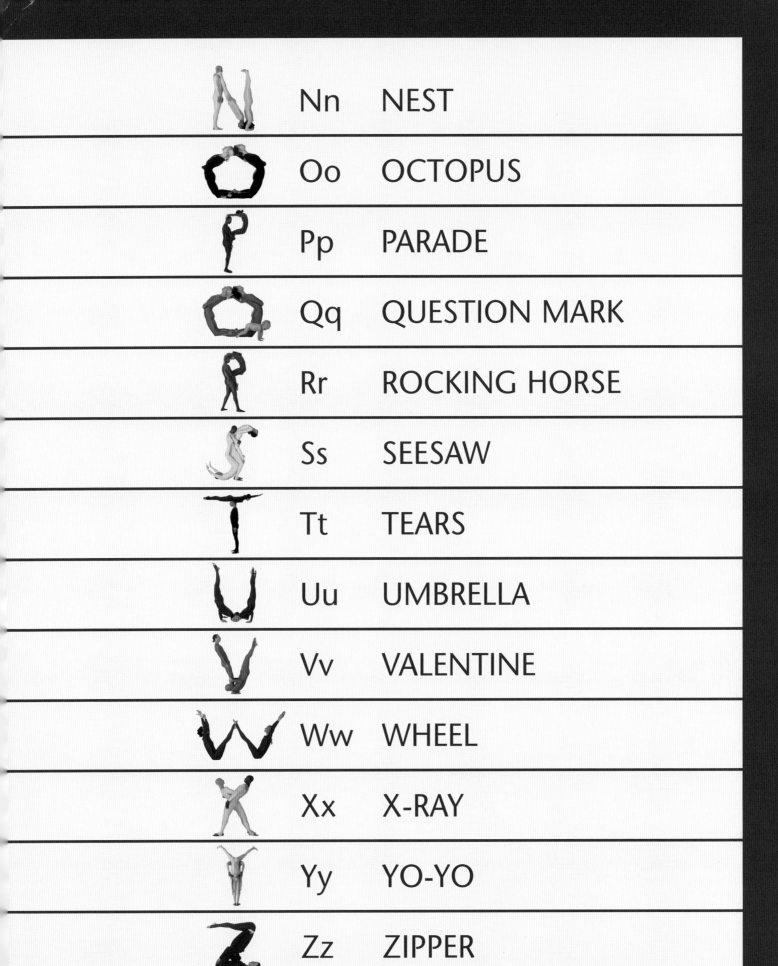

| | | |
|---|---|---|
| | Nn | NEST |
| | Oo | OCTOPUS |
| | Pp | PARADE |
| | Qq | QUESTION MARK |
| | Rr | ROCKING HORSE |
| | Ss | SEESAW |
| | Tt | TEARS |
| | Uu | UMBRELLA |
| | Vv | VALENTINE |
| | Ww | WHEEL |
| | Xx | X-RAY |
| | Yy | YO-YO |
| | Zz | ZIPPER |

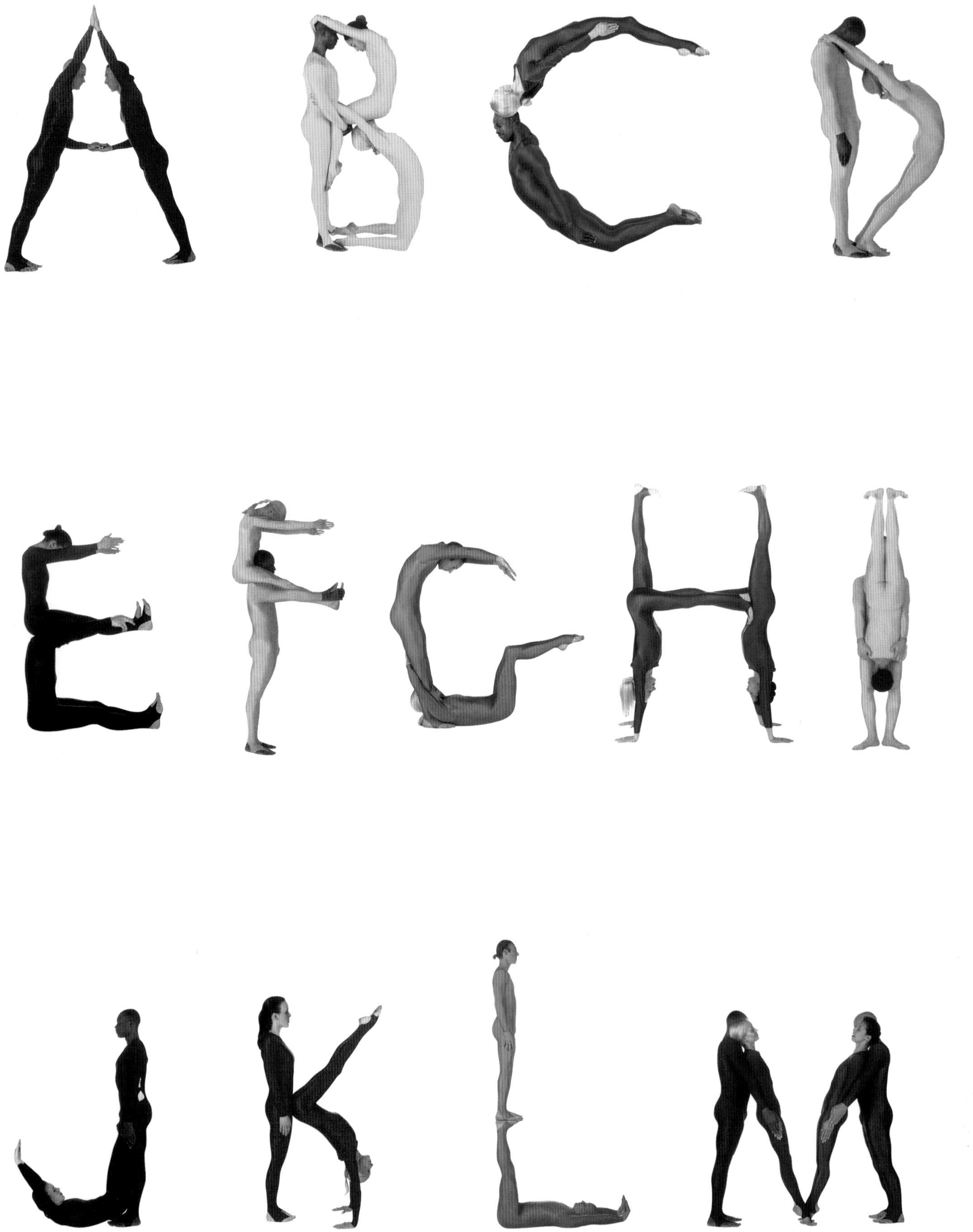